GO, JADE, GO!

written by Tony and Lauren Dungy
with Nathan Whitaker

illustrated by
Vanessa Brantley Newton

Ready-to-Read

Simon Spotlight
New York   London   Toronto   Sydney   New Delhi

SIMON SPOTLIGHT
An imprint of Simon & Schuster Children's Publishing Division
1230 Avenue of the Americas, New York, New York 10020
Text copyright © 2013 by Tony Dungy and Lauren Dungy
Illustrations copyright © 2013 by Vanessa Brantley Newton
Published in association with the literacy agency of Legacy, LLC, Winter Park, FL 32789
All rights reserved, including the right of reproduction in whole or in part in any form.
SIMON SPOTLIGHT, READY-TO-READ, and colophon are registered trademarks of
Simon & Schuster, Inc. For information about special discounts for bulk purchases, please contact
Simon & Schuster Special Sales at 1-866-506-1949 or business@simonandschuster.com.
The Simon & Schuster Speakers Bureau can bring authors to your live event.
For more information or to book an event contact the Simon & Schuster Speakers Bureau at
1-866-248-3049 or visit our website at www.simonspeakers.com
Manufactured in the United States of America 0613 LAK
First Edition 10 9 8 7 6 5 4 3 2 1
Cataloging-in-Publication Data for this book available from the Library of Congress.
ISBN 978-1-4424-5466-8 (pbk)
ISBN 978-1-4424-5467-5 (hc)
ISBN 978-1-4424-5468-2 (eBook)

JADE'S DAY AT THE TRACK

"This is boring."
Justin's words were loud,
but not loud enough to hear
over the roar of the crowd.

The runners took off
racing around the track.
There were kids everywhere,
running and jumping.
Jade went by . . . *whoosh!*

"Run, Jade, run!" yelled Jordan.
"You can do it!" said Dad.
"Go, Jade!" cheered Mom.

Justin wasn't cheering.
He wasn't even watching.
He leaned his head on his hand
and hoped the races would end
soon.

BACK AT HOME

Jade got a drink out of the fridge.
"You were great today," said Jordan.
"Yes, you were," said Dad.

"We are really blessed," said Mom.
"All of our children are so talented
in different ways."

Justin didn't say anything.
He was sitting by himself,
staring out the window.

Mom looked at Justin.
"Didn't you have fun today?"
asked Mom.

"Not really," replied Justin.
"All I did was watch
Jade run around."

"It was fun, Justin," said Dad.
"It was great to be there to cheer
for Jade."

"Well, it wasn't fun for me.
All I did was get hot and tired,"
Justin complained.

BIG BROTHER HELPS

Later, Justin and Ruby went outside.
Ruby kept nudging Justin
with her ball.
Justin usually loved playing outside,
but he didn't feel like it today.

Jordan came outside to play
with Justin and Ruby.

"Hi, Justin," Jordan said.
"Want to throw the ball?"
"No, thanks," said Justin.

"Want to go ride bikes?"
"No, thanks," said Justin.

"What's the matter?" asked Jordan. "I wish I was good at something that made everyone cheer for me," said Justin.

"Remember, like Mom and Dad said, we're all good at something," Jordan told him.

"You're great at drawing and art.
Your pictures are all over
the house!"
Justin nodded.

"And everyone was happy for me
when I won a ribbon
in the science fair," said Jordan.

Justin nodded again.
"You're right," said Justin.

"So you should be happy for Jade. Everyone is happy for us when we do things well," said Jordan. "You just have to do your best."

Justin looked away, thinking.
Then suddenly a huge smile
spread across Justin's face.
He had an idea!

A BANNER DAY

Everyone was excited.
They were waiting
for Jade's track meet to begin.

Justin wasn't complaining at all.
He was holding something in his
hand. It was a surprise for Jade.

On the field Jade was warming up,
and her family called out to her.
"Do your best, Jade!" yelled Mom.
"We love you, Jade!" Dad shouted.

"Yay, Jade!" Jordan yelled.
"Look, everybody!" shouted Justin.

He started to unroll a big sign
and unroll . . .

GO!

and unroll . . .

and unroll.

Mom and Dad hugged Justin.
Jordan grinned and
bumped fists with Justin.
"Good job, little buddy,"
Jordan said.
Everybody cheered as Jade
got set to race.

Just then Jade looked up
and saw Justin's big sign.
"Thanks, Justin. You rock!"
she called.
"Yay, Jade!" called Justin.
"Go, go, go!"

Whoosh went Jade as she ran by.
Justin had made his best sign.
Jade ran her best race.
It was the best day ever
at the track!